YULETIDE TERROR

PORSHA GARRETT

INTRODUCTION

Welcome to a chilling world where the joyful holiday season transforms into a time of terror and dread. Within these pages, you will encounter short horror stories set amidst the twinkling lights and cheerful festivities of Christmas. From ancient Yuletide curses to sinister encounters with otherworldly beings, these tales will haunt your imagination and instill a sense of unease in the midst of the season's merriment. Prepare to delve into a realm where the warmth of the hearth is overshadowed by the icy grip of fear, and where the familiar carols of Christmas take on an ominous tone. Embrace the spirit of the macabre this holiday season, if you dare.

STORY 1

GNOME SWEET GNOME

Natalie looked forward to the Christmas Jubilee every year, she absolutely loved everything about Christmas the songs, the sweet treats, putting up her Christmas tree. She practically waited all year for this one day. The Anderson Farm hosted a huge function with Christmas displays, holiday treats and even a beautiful drive through light show. Natalie planned the perfect date with her boyfriend Nate, though Nate was not a fan of Christmas he agreed to go and make Natalie happy.

As the evening approached, Natalie put on her Christmas attire and waited for Nate to pick her up, legend had it that the Anderson farms gnomes were more than just decoration and some had claimed to see them move in their own, Natalie was looking forward to possibly catching a glimpse.

Natalie was quickly brought back to reality with the honking of Nate's car horn, quickly grabbing her things, Natalie rushed out the door and hopped in the car. " Hey babe, are you super excited" Natalie was grinning from ear to ear. Nate just looked at her, she could tell he was not thrilled. " I promise you'll love it!"

Natalie decided to keep to herself the legend of the gnomes, she didn't want to ruin the chances of Nate not coming or thinking she was losing it, as they'd only been dating close to a year. As they walked hand in hand sipping hot chocolate, Natalie screamed " look at the lights Nate" in the distance she could see flashing lights that all moved in sync with rhythmic bass she could feel through her feet.

"We have to drive through it" Natalie screeched. "$40" Nate looked at Natalie, " you wanna see lights, I'll string some up at home! This is ridiculous." But Nate couldn't resist Natalie's puppy dog eyes as she looked at him in disappointment. Needless to say, he bought the tickets.

As they drove slowly through the dazzling display of lights, Nate griped and groaned about every penny he was spending. "I can't believe I spent forty bucks for us to stare at blinking Christmas lights. I could've hung a string of lights around our living room for cheaper," he grumbled.

Natalie tried to ignore his complaints and focused on the beautiful displays. Suddenly, she spotted a group of garden gnomes sitting beneath a giant, twinkling Christmas tree. "Look at the gnomes, Nate!" she exclaimed.

"Those creepy little things? They're giving me the creeps," Nate said, rolling his eyes. "Who would even think of putting those in a Christmas display? They're so... dumb!" He laughed, pointing at the gnomes from the car window.

Just as he was about to make another sarcastic comment, the car behind them began to honk their horn, flashing their lights. Startled, Nate fumbled with the wheel, swerving slightly before getting back on track.

Finally, they reached home. Despite Nate's incessant complaining, Natalie was still glowing with holiday cheer. She gave Nate a quick peck on his cheek before darting into their home, leaving Nate alone in the car.

The following morning, Natalie woke up to find Nate missing from their bed. Frowning, she searched the house and finally found him in their bedroom, tangled in a mess of Christmas lights. His mouth was agape, eyes wide open in surprise. A piece of paper lay next to him, reading "Merry Christmas."

Natalie's heart pounded in her chest as she took in the gory scene. Nate's skin was pale and cold, his hands still clutching the Christmas lights as if he had been trying to unravel himself. The once beautiful Christmas lights were now a terrifying reminder of the horrifying event from the previous night.

She remembered Nate's disdain for the gnomes, his ridicule of the Christmas displays, and his complaints about the money he had spent. As her mind raced, she couldn't help but think about the legends of the gnomes she had kept to herself. Could it be that they were not just legends? Was Nate's fate somehow connected to the ridicule he had thrown at them?

As fear gripped her, Natalie could only wish she had never dragged him to the Christmas Jubilee.

STORY 2

DRUMMER BOY

From a tender age Jarvis dreamed of being a famous drummer, he used to break branches off of trees and hit everything in sight. For his fifth birthday he was gifted a pair of drum sticks, which had his mother rethinking the gift.

Fast forward Jarvis is approaching his sixteenth birthday and dreams of nothing more than an actual drum set. Jarvis sees how hard his mother is working to put food on the table so he can only wish that all the overtime is for his drum set.

" Excuse me, do these come in a size 8 Lucinda." Jarvis's mother could barely hear nor concentrate, the atmosphere was full of children crying, shopping carts clinging together, the ridiculously loud Christmas music and the yelling of unruly customers. " Let me check in back miss" as the customer just stood there holding the shoe and chewing her gum as if she was working out her jaws for a marathon.

Lucinda couldn't wait to step away for just a breather, searching frantically for a size 8 she notices a piece of paper sticking out from under the shelve, " LIMITED TIME ONLY " she begins to read as her co worker sneaks up behind her. " So are you going?" She whispers. Lucinda shrugs her shoulders " I don't think I'll get off in time." " That's a shame" Lucinda's coworker replies " because they had that drum set Jarvis has been eyeing for super cheap."

" Are you serious! Jarvis would be the happiest 16 year old in the world if I can get that drum set for him." Lucinda rushes out with the shoes for the rude customer and quickly gets back to work, but all she can do was keep checking the time. Lucinda just had to get to this special store before they closed because tomorrow was Jarvis's special day.

Counting the last of the day's deposit Lucinda hurry's to grab her things and dashes out the door. She pulls out the flyer the double the address, but as she's getting closer she's noticing there are no stores. " This can't be right" as she's checking all the addresses they appear to be matching so she keeps walking.

Further down the dim lit alleyway Lucinda sees flashing lights, she clutches her purse and starts to make a mad dash in wishes to make it in before closing. But as she approaches the worker is just flipping the open sign to closed. Lucinda starts yelling loudly enough to be heard through the glass, " please I just need one thing" the worker shakes their head and points to the sign.

" Please, it's for my son's birthday " Lucinda starts pointing to the drum set she can see behind the worker, " The drum set, I need that." Lucinda starts crying and falls to the ground. Tired, exhausted and now wet as it begins to rain, Lucinda now feels like a failure. If only she worked faster, if only she counted the money quicker. Now dwelling in self pity.

Lucinda hears a click. She looks up and sees the door opening.

" Come in child" the worker who appeared to be too old to be working helped Lucinda up off the wet ground and guided her into the store. " Is this what you want my child" slowly walking around the drum set, Lucinda watched as the old woman's finger ran alongside the well polished brass. " Yes please, it's for my son's sixteenth birthday." The old woman stopped abruptly and turned around " 16 you say " the old woman's face begin to light up as if she'd won the lottery.

Not paying any mind Lucinda crying and pleading replied " yes" with her head hanging low. " Consider this my gift for your dearest son my child" Lucinda looked up " what " the old woman began boxing up pieces. " Take it, as a gift for we only turn 16 once." Lucinda began thanking the old woman over and over she couldn't believe this was happening.

The day had finally come, Jarvis comes running down the stairs and sitting in the middle of the living room wrapped with a bow

was his new drum set. " Mom" Jarvis runs over and with so much excitement jumps into his mother's arms. " Mom I can't believe it! Really is this for me?"
Lucinda sheds tears of happiness. " yes son, you deserve it."

As the days turned into weeks Jarvis was consumed with the drum set, he didn't leave the house. He barely ate or hung out with his friends. Lucinda tried everything, making his favorite meals inviting over friends, but nothing could take his attention away from the drum set.

Lucinda grew increasingly worried. Jarvis was not himself. He was withdrawing, his eyes were hollow, and he showed no interest in anything except the drum set. He would bang on the drums for hours on end, the rhythm growing louder and faster each day. His once gentle touch turned aggressive, the beats echoing through the house with an eerie melody.

One day, Lucinda decided to return to the antique store from where she had gotten the drum set. Walking down the familiar alley, she was surprised to find the store was no longer there. It was as if the store had never existed. The quaint building had turned into an empty building. She asked the neighboring shopkeepers, but they all seemed to have no recollection of the antique store or the old woman.

With growing dread, Lucinda started researching the drum set. Hours turned into days as she scoured the internet, libraries, and archives. Her search led her to a tragic story of a young boy from the 1950s. The boy was a prodigy drummer who yearned for fame and fortune. His wish came true when he was discovered by a talent scout. But the fame came at a great cost. The boy was exploited, worked to exhaustion, and died tragically young. Legend said his spirit was trapped in his drum set, the instrument of his destruction.

Lucinda knew she had to free her son from the curse. She called upon a local spiritualist, who guided her through a complex ritual. They lit candles, burned sage, and chanted incantations.

Jarvis watched in a daze from the corner of the room, his eyes never leaving the drum set.

The ritual seemed to work. Jarvis blinked, as if coming out of a trance. He looked around, confused and tired. His mother rushed to him, holding him close. They both cried, relief washing over them.

The next day, Lucinda and Jarvis decided to get rid of the drum set. They took it to a remote field, doused it in gasoline, and set it aflame. The fire roared, consuming the cursed instrument. They watched as the flames danced and flickered, the eerie melody of the drums disappearing with the smoke.

"Are you okay?" Lucinda asked, wrapping an arm around Jarvis.

"I think I am," Jarvis replied, his voice barely above a whisper. He looked at the burning drum set, his eyes reflecting the dancing flames. "I think I'm finally free."

From then on, things started to return to normal. Jarvis went back to school, started eating properly, and hung out with his friends. The hollow look in his eyes disappeared, replaced with the spark of life Lucinda had missed so much.

In the end, Lucinda learned a valuable lesson about the cost of desires and the importance of freedom. She also learned the lengths she would go to save her child. As she watched Jarvis return to his normal life, she couldn't help but feel a wave of relief. Her son was back, and the nightmare was finally over.

STORY 3

THE CURSED TELEVISION SET

James had always been close to grandmother Edna. She had raised him after his parents died when he was just a child. Now, as an adult, he made it a point to visit her every week, spending hours chatting with her about the good old days. However, there was one thing that always bothered him during his visits—the ancient, clunky TV that sat in the corner of her living room. It seemed to belong to a bygone era, and the picture quality was abysmal.

As Christmas approached, James decided to do something about it. Determined to give his beloved grandmother a more modern and enjoyable viewing experience, he purchased a brand-new smart TV and installed it in her living room as a surprise. Edna was overjoyed with the gift, and for the first few weeks, she seemed to revel in the crisp, clear images and endless entertainment options.

But as the days passed, James noticed a change in his grandmother. She became increasingly fixated on the TV, spending long hours staring at the screen in silence. At first, he dismissed it as the novelty of her new gadget, but soon he realized something was not right. One evening, as he visited her, he found her sitting in front of the TV, tears streaming down her face.

"Granny, what's wrong?" James asked, rushing to her side.

She turned to him, her eyes filled with a mixture of sadness and fear. "James, I saw... I saw myself on the TV. It showed me things from long ago, things I thought I'd forgotten."

James was taken aback. "What do you mean, Granny? You're just watching shows on the new TV, that's all."

But Edna shook her head. "No, James, you don't understand. It's not just shows. It's memories, my memories. They're coming back to haunt me."

James tried to reassure her, but the fear in her eyes lingered. He stayed with her that night, keeping her company until she eventually fell asleep.

The following week, James received a frantic call from his grandmother. She was babbling incoherently about the TV, begging him to come over. Alarmed, he rushed to her house, his heart pounding in his chest. When he arrived, he found the front door ajar and the house filled with an eerie silence.

"Granny?" he called out, his voice echoing through the empty rooms.

He found her in the living room, huddled in front of the TV, her eyes wide with terror. "James, it's happening again. I can't stop it," she whispered.

Before he could respond, the TV screen flickered and distorted, and to James's horror, he saw fleeting images of his grandmother's past flashing across the screen. He saw her as a young girl, playing in the fields near her childhood home. He saw her as a young woman, laughing with friends at a long-forgotten party. And then, without warning, the screen seemed to ripple and warp, as if it were a liquid surface.

"Granny, what's happening?" James cried out, reaching for her.

But before he could reach her, his grandmother was drawn towards the TV as if by an invisible force. She vanished into the screen, leaving James standing there in shock, his mind reeling with disbelief.

For days, James was plagued by the traumatic sight of his grandmother being sucked into the TV. He couldn't sleep, he couldn't eat, and he couldn't shake the feeling that something sinister had taken hold of his grandmother and dragged her into the depths of the television.

Determined to unravel the mystery, James delved into his grandmother's past. He pored over old photo albums, letters, and mementos, searching for any clue that could explain the strange occurrences. As he dug deeper, he uncovered a dark family secret that had been buried for decades—a secret that had tormented his grandmother throughout her life.

It was a cold, rainy night when James returned to his grandmother's house, armed with newfound knowledge and a sense of urgency. He switched on the TV, hoping to find some connection between its strange behavior and the family secret. As he flipped through the channels, he stumbled upon a static-filled image that sent a shiver down his spine.

The screen flickered, and for a moment, James saw a familiar face staring back at him—it was his grandmother, but she appeared younger, haunted, and trapped within the confines of the TV. Her eyes bore into his, pleading for help as if she were reaching out from another dimension.

A chill crept down James's spine as the room grew colder, and the lights flickered ominously. He felt a presence behind him, a presence that seemed to emanate from the TV itself. He turned around slowly, his heart pounding in his chest, and was met with a sight that sent terror coursing through his veins.

Standing before him was a spectral figure, a twisted, distorted version of his grandmother, her features contorted in agony. Her eyes glowed with an otherworldly light, and her voice echoed through the room, a haunting whisper that seemed to come from everywhere and nowhere at once.

"James, help me," she moaned, her voice filled with a profound sadness.

Paralyzed with fear, James stumbled backward, his mind struggling to comprehend the impossible sight before him. He felt a cold, unseen hand grip his shoulder, and he realized with mounting horror that the boundary between the real world and the TV was beginning to blur.

In a desperate bid for escape, James lunged for the remote control and frantically tried to turn off the TV. But as he pressed the power button, the screen erupted into a blinding, pulsating light, and he was engulfed in a whirlwind of memories and emotions that weren't his own.

He found himself tumbling through a surreal landscape, a place where time and space seemed to fold in on themselves. He caught fleeting glimpses of his grandmother's past, her joys and sorrows intertwining with his own, and he felt an overwhelming sense of despair and longing.

Just as suddenly as it had begun, the tumultuous journey came to an abrupt halt, and James found himself standing in a shadowy realm that bore a twisted resemblance to his grandmother's living room. The TV loomed before him, a menacing presence that seemed to pulse with a malevolent energy.

And then, from the depths of the darkness, he heard a mournful wail that pierced through the air, a sound that seemed to echo with centuries of anguish and despair. As the wail intensified, James realized with a sinking heart that it was his grandmother's voice, trapped within the confines of the TV, crying out for release from the endless torment

STORY 4

THE UNSEEN GUEST

In the dead of winter, nestled within the vast, snow-cloaked wilderness, sat a small cabin. A beacon of warmth amid the icy desolation, it was home to Andrew, a rugged, middle-aged man, and his family: his wife, Clara, and their two children, Emily and Sam. They lived a simple life, isolated from the rest of the world, their existence marked by the changing seasons and the rhythms of nature.

On a frigid Christmas Eve, with the wind howling like a pack of hungry wolves outside, a knock resounded through the cabin. Surprised by the unexpected visitor, Andrew cautiously opened the door to reveal a man, seemingly on the edge of exhaustion, his eyes carrying an enigmatic sadness. He introduced himself as Elias and asked, with a shiver in his voice, for shelter from the cold. Moved by the spirit of the holiday, the family welcomed him into their home.

Elias was a quiet guest, his presence subtle and unimposing. He thanked Andrew and Clara for their kindness, and shared stories of his travels, his words painting vivid landscapes and bustling cities far removed from the family's secluded life. All was well, and Christmas Eve unfurled with the comfort of tradition and newfound camaraderie.

However, as the night grew darker, strange occurrences began to manifest. The wind, once a mere whisper, rose into a furious gale. The fire, which had been crackling merrily in the hearth, flickered ominously, casting long, monstrous shadows on the cabin walls. A sense of unease permeated the air, an unseen guest veiling the festivities with an aura of dread.

The clocks chimed midnight, and the Christmas tree, previously gleaming with cheerful lights, abruptly went dark. The cabin plunged into an unnatural silence, pierced only by the erratic beating of their hearts. Suddenly,

the youngest, Sam, let out a terrified shriek.
His favorite toy, a wooden horse, had
inexplicably burst into flames. As Andrew
rushed to extinguish the fire, Elias, his face as
pale as the snow outside, murmured an
apology.

With trepidation etched on his face, Elias
confessed to his curse. He was a wanderer,
doomed to carry chaos and destruction
wherever he went. He had hoped, foolishly,
that the curse might spare them on this holy
night. He was wrong. The family listened in
disbelief, their cozy Christmas Eve turned into
a nightmare.

The night wore on, their cabin transformed into
a maelic maw of horror. Objects flew across
rooms, windows shattered without cause, and
chilling whispers echoed through the corridors.
Fear gripped Andrew's heart, but he knew he
had to protect his family.

In the midst of the chaos, Andrew, fueled by
desperation, challenged Elias. "You brought
this upon us," he accused, "you need to end
it!". Elias, his eyes filled with regret, nodded.

He explained that the curse could be transferred to another, willing to accept it. He had carried the burden for centuries, unable to find a reprieve.

Tension hung heavy in the room as Andrew grappled with the impossible decision. He thought of Clara, her face pale and drawn with terror. He thought of Emily and Sam, their young lives marred by this night of horror. He thought of their tranquil existence, now shattered by the unseen guest.

With a heavy heart, Andrew made his decision. He declared his willingness to bear the curse, to protect his family from further harm. Elias, filled with gratitude and sorrow, performed the ancient ritual. The curse lifted from him, manifesting as a dark, swirling mist before it descended onto Andrew. The cabin returned to normal, the chaos subsiding as quickly as it had begun.

As the first light of Christmas morning filtered through the broken windows, Elias, freed from his curse, thanked Andrew for his sacrifice and left, disappearing into the snowy wilderness.

Andrew, now the carrier of the curse, embraced his family, their relief tainted with the knowledge of the burden he now bore.

For the rest of his life, Andrew lived with the curse, forever the unseen guest in their home. But within the horror, they found an odd sense of peace. Their love for each other, strengthened by the ordeal, became their sanctuary. Their lives, though marred by chaos, were bound by an unbreakable bond. And the cabin in the woods, though forever touched by the terrifying events of that Christmas Eve, remained their home, their beacon of warmth amid the icy desolation.

STORY 5

THE CAROL OF THE DEAD

In the quaint, snow-laden town of Harrowsfield, nestled in the heart of Pennsylvania, a chilling curse descended each Christmas. A curse that turned the joyous festival into a macabre event of death and despair. The town would relive the same Christmas Day, each time ending with the brutal demise of all its inhabitants at the hands of spectral carolers. The chilling echoes of their eerie hymns would be the last thing the people heard before an icy hand of death swept over them.

A group of survivors, thrown together by chance and the deadly circumstance, discovered the curse was tied to a sinful act committed by the town's founder, a man named Ebenezer Harrow. They were the only ones spared from the spectral carolers' wrath, a mystery that linked them together.

The group was diverse, each carrying their own burdens and secrets. There was Mayor Thompson, the town's leader, a man of courage and integrity. Emily, the quiet librarian with a love for history and puzzles. Father O'Malley, the old, wise parish priest. And finally, two teenagers, Jake and Molly, who had lost their families to the curse.

As the ghostly echoes of "God Rest Ye Merry Gentlemen" reverberated through the frosty air, the survivors gathered in the town library, the only place they found safe from the spectral carolers.

"It's Harrow, it has to be," Emily said, her fingers tracing the age-old documents about the town's history. "He did something... something that has cursed us all."

They delved deep into the town's past, uncovering dark secrets that were better left buried. Ebenezer Harrow, they discovered, was a ruthless man. To establish Harrowsfield, he had orchestrated the violent displacement of a local tribe, slaughtering men, women, and children during their sacred winter solstice celebration. The final piece of the puzzle fell into place when Emily unearthed an ancient tribal song, eerily similar to the haunting melody of the spectral carolers.

"It's a curse," Father O'Malley concluded, his voice trembling with age and fear. "A curse for the blood Harrow spilled. A curse we relive every Christmas."

The group realized they had been spared because their ancestors were not part of Harrow's heinous act. But knowledge was not enough; they needed to break the curse. The solution, they hypothesized, was in the song—the tribal song of forgiveness and renewal. They needed to perform it on Christmas Day, as a plea for forgiveness, in the very square where the massacre had taken place.

The night before Christmas, the survivors prepared. Fear was in their hearts, but so was hope. They had one chance to break the curse and free their town from the eternal cycle of death and rebirth.

As dawn broke on Christmas Day, the spectral carolers appeared, their ghostly figures materializing amidst the falling snow. The haunting melody began to fill the air. But this time, it was met with another song. The survivors, standing firmly in the town square, began to sing. Their voices, filled with remorse and pleading, intertwined with the spectral melody, creating a hauntingly beautiful harmony.

The spectral carolers paused, their icy gaze falling upon the singers. For a moment, everything was still. Then, slowly, the spectral figures began to fade, their song growing fainter until it finally disappeared. The survivors' song of forgiveness echoed through the empty square, and as the final notes drifted away, they felt a profound sense of relief.

As the sun rose higher, Harrowsfield was quiet, filled with a peace it hadn't known for centuries. The curse was broken. No longer would Christmas bring death. From that year forward, the town celebrated Christmas with a new tradition—a song of forgiveness and renewal, a reminder of the past they had overcome.

And so, the survivors had not only saved themselves but also their town. They had uncovered a dark past and, in doing so, had given Harrowsfield a future. It was a Christmas they would never forget, the Christmas when they silenced the Carol of the Dead.

STORY 6

THE CHRISTMAS DOLL

Makenzie Hughes had always been the darling of her eccentric Uncle Everett. A collector of the strange, the bizarre, the uncanny, Uncle Everett had bestowed upon Makenzie an unusual Christmas gift—an antique dollhouse. It was a grand, Victorian miniature, its attention to detail astonishing. But the real surprise lay within the dollhouse—a collection of dolls that bore an uncanny resemblance to her family members.

Makenzie was both fascinated and unnerved by the dolls. Uncle Everett merely chuckled at her apprehension, his eyes twinkling with a peculiar gleam. "A unique piece, isn't it?" he'd said, his words echoing in Makenzie's mind as she scrutinized the dolls.

The fascination turned into terror when the doll resembling her younger brother, Sammy, fell from the dollhouse's tiny stairs, its porcelain head shattering into pieces. The very next day, Sammy fell down the staircase of their actual home, his head injury mirroring the doll's fate.

One by one, the dolls met gruesome ends. Aunt Clara's doll drowned in the dollhouse's tiny bathtub, Uncle Bill's doll was found in the dollhouse's miniature fireplace, charred beyond recognition. And, horrifyingly, their real-life counterparts suffered the same fate.

Realization dawned on Makenzie. The dollhouse was not just a toy; it was a harbinger of death. And her own doll, a miniature Makenzie in a red Christmas dress, was still inside.

Fear gripped her heart, but she knew she couldn't succumb. She had to solve the mystery of the dollhouse before her own doll met its end. As the only one who understood the dollhouse's deadly power, it was up to her to save herself.

Makenzie began her investigation, delving into the history of the dollhouse. She discovered it was made by a toymaker named Jasper Moray, who was notorious for his involvement in the occult. It was said that Moray had the power to trap souls in his creations, imbuing them with a life of their own.

Time was running out. Makenzie could feel an ominous presence around her doll in the dollhouse. She knew she had to break the curse. Her research led her to an ancient ritual meant to free trapped souls. It required her to confront the spirit controlling the dollhouse.

On a cold Christmas Eve, Makenzie sat in front of the dollhouse, her heart pounding. The house was eerily quiet, her unfortunate family members unaware of the supernatural drama unfolding. With a deep breath, she began the ritual.

She confronted the spirit of Jasper Moray, her voice steady, demanding him to release her family from his twisted game. The dollhouse shook, the miniature chandelier swinging violently. But Makenzie did not falter. She continued the ritual, her voice rising above the supernatural storm.

And then, silence. The shaking stopped. Makenzie looked at the dollhouse, her heart pounding. Her doll still stood, untouched. She felt a wave of relief wash over her. She had done it. She had broken the curse.

From that day forward, the dollhouse was nothing more than a collection of wood and porcelain, its deadly power extinguished. Makenzie had saved herself, and in doing so, she had saved her family from further tragedy.

"The Christmas Doll" became a chilling reminder of the Christmas Makenzie would never forget—the Christmas she stared into the eyes of death and emerged victorious.